The Buddha and the Terrorist

BUDDHA
and the
TERRORIST

by

SATISH KUMAR

with a foreword by
Thomas Moore

and an afterword by
Allan Hunt Badiner

ALGONQUIN BOOKS OF CHAPEL HILL   2006

Published by

ALGONQUIN BOOKS OF CHAPEL HILL
Post Office Box 2225
Chapel Hill, North Carolina 27515-2225

a division of
WORKMAN PUBLISHING
225 Varick Street
New York, New York 10014

Library of Congress Cataloging-in-Publication Data

Satish Kumar, 1936–
    The Buddha and the terrorist / Satish Kumar. — 1st ed.
      p. cm.
    ISBN-13: 978-1-56512-520-9; ISBN-10: 1-56512-520-7
    1. Angulimala — Fiction.   I. Title.
PR6069.A77B83 2006
  823'.92 — dc22   2006045861

10 9 8 7 6 5 4 3 2 1
First Edition

CONTENTS

◈ ☉ ◈

FOREWORD

Holy Terror
by Thomas Moore

It is often said, accurately, that violence begets violence. There is a virus buried deep in all violence that is contagious, that inspires an equally brutal and mindless response. A terrorist blows up a bus, and an army comes out to settle the score. This exchange of violence and this contagion of terror have been handed down for eons from family to family and from nation to nation. It is a chain of terror made up of people gone amok with anger and those just as disturbed with their feelings of virtue and righteous vengeance.

But there is good news. The Gospel of Jesus, the Dharma of Buddha, the Tao of Lao Tzu, and the *tariqa,* or way of love, in Sufism all teach that you can let go of your grip on this chain. You can be free of it. When obscene violence interrupts your life, you don't have to respond with virtuous, justified, and reasonable force. You can choose not to be part of the destructive cycle, and that choice not to participate is a first step toward peace.

But to step outside the circle of terror you have to do something quite unreasonable. You have to forfeit vengeance and abandon all reasonable expectations that the majority of your community, friends, and family may take for granted. You will probably have to go it alone and trust your spiritual instincts. You may appear passive and weak. Only you know the inner courage needed to overcome habits of vengeance and punishment that are assumed to be right and virtuous.

You need your spiritual instincts because the way out of violence depends on a great and penetrating vision. You have to understand radically that terrorism of all kinds is an insanity, whether it is the work of a band of renegades or the more sanctioned and public action of an army. You have to understand that violence, even when calculated, is the expression of a pained and twisted soul. It is the work of a spirit or urge that takes over a person or a people and blinds them to human solidarity and community. Your job, in the spirit of the Buddha and Jesus, is to calm the souls of everyone involved.

At root, the word "terror" means to quiver or tremble, like a bird in the hand or a leaf in the wind on a tree. It's more than fear. Essentially it is a profound awareness of the power of life itself. A psalm from the Bible says, "The Lord most high is terrible." And at the consecration of a church the choir sings, "Terrible is this place." (In this old usage, *terrible* and *terror* are different forms of the same word.)

The Lord, the source of life, truly inspires terror because life is so mysterious and overwhelming and because it offers so much vitality and so much death. According to a classic definition, the holy is *mysterium tremendum et fascinans,* that is, a mystery that makes you tremble and fascinates you. The ultimate terror is a stark realization of the holiness and awesomeness of life.

But everything is subject to human neurosis and psychosis. It's quite proper to tremble at the sight and feel of nature's beauty and power, but it's a travesty for anyone to force another to tremble at the sight of weapons and savagery. The most beneficial of things can be twisted into something dangerous and ugly. When that happens, we usually add an "ism" to the word. Community becomes communism, nationality becomes nationalism, and terror becomes terrorism.

Terrorism is a sacrilege, and our task is to respond by restoring the holiness of life's power.

Humans are always trying to usurp the power of life for their own purposes. In the National Museum of Ireland you can see and hear ancient and elaborate horns that were blown before battle to terrorize an enemy, and on the American plains warriors would deck themselves in war paint before fighting to instill fright. A husband raises his voice and smashes furniture to terrorize his wife.

It is tempting to respond to savage terrorism with violence that looks more civilized. We cover over our terrorism with a veneer of patriotism, piety, and justifications. But beneath all the formality we are blowing our horns like the Celts, convincing ourselves of our innocence as we arm our weapons.

Religions explain the human love of war as a misplaced and misunderstood version of the struggle with ignorance and blind passion. Many in

Islam would say that jihad is primarily a spiritual battle for insight and tranquility. Jesus said that he brought a sword, but clearly he wasn't talking about a literal fight. He also told his companion Peter to put his literal sword in its sheath.

Renouncing terrorism doesn't mean that you become passive and fainthearted. It means that you have the imagination, the self-possession, and the strength to reconstruct terrorism as awe at the beauty and power of life. You become a spiritual warrior. You discover that it takes far more courage to transform the impulse toward justified violence into the embrace of a supposed adversary. The real battle is to overcome self-interest and the tendency to split the world into friends and enemies.

Both Jesus and the Buddha refuse to participate in a world so divided. Jesus says, "Love your enemy," and the Buddha befriends a bloodthirsty criminal. These examples upset the "natural" urge to respond to terrorism with massive violence. But that is the nature of a religious and spiritual sensibility: It offers an alternative to raw and violent passion. It sees things differently. It has a radical mission to restore human community whenever it has broken down. The religious spirit transforms fear into awe and violence into compassionate action. We can begin to cultivate small acts of compassion right now.

In his last sermon the Buddha simply held up a flower for contemplation. He is identified with the lotus flower, a delicate but tough plant that has a long and firm nourishing root. The terrorist, making a gross mistake about the nature of power, instead holds a gun over his head to inspire fear. Our task as spiritual people is to restore the power symbolized by a flower and cure the weakness symbolized by a weapon.

The Sufi poet Rumi tells of a great warrior, Ali. Once, he got the best of a knight and drew his sword on the man. The man spat at him. Ali dropped his weapon and helped the man up. The man was confused. Why did Ali do this?

"I am God's lion, not the lion of passion," Ali explained. "When the wind of personal reaction comes, I do not go along with it. The poison of your spit has become the honey of friendship."

The Buddha and the Terrorist

❋

INTRODUCTION

❖ ⊙ ❖

The Story of Angulimala

The story of Angulimala is to be found in the
Buddhist scriptures. I learned it from Gunaratna,
a Sri Lankan Buddhist monk, and then from a
Tibetan lama. Later I read the story in *The Life of
the Buddha* by Bhikkhu Nanamoli, and in *Old Path
White Clouds* by Thich Nhat Hanh. In the classic
Buddhist version, Angulimala is described as being
born into a high caste, a Brahmin family, his father
being called Gagga and mother Mantani, but as
part of the oral culture of India, the story has
many versions.

In the version which I learned from my mother in my early childhood, Angulimala is born as an outcaste, an untouchable. He suffers from degradation and discrimination, which turns him into a rebel. He uses violent means to seek power and gain control. This version of the story better explains why someone who was named Ahimsaka ("The Nonviolent One") by his parents takes up the sword and becomes a murderer, nicknamed Angulimala ("Wearer of a Finger Necklace"). In retelling the story, I have preferred to use this version.

In the Buddhist version, it is not clear why a Brahmin boy born into a privileged caste should go on such a rampage. I hope my Buddhist friends will not mind this mixing of the two accounts.

My aim in writing this story has been two-fold: firstly, to show that there is another way, a more effective way, to overcome terror than the way of meeting fire with fire; and secondly, to introduce Buddhist philosophy, as I understand it, through a narrative. In our troubled times we need to be courageous, creative, and compassionate, and to exercise our imagination in order to build a better future. Therefore the story of Angulimala is as relevant today as ever.

I have used Pali spellings of names where these are not already in popular English usage, but otherwise have used the popular Sanskrit spellings as in the Oxford Dictionary.

I am grateful to June Mitchell, my wife, for listening to my retelling and for being my scribe and editor. I am also grateful to my friends Lindsay Clarke, John Lane, John Moat, Stephen Batchelor, and Chris Cullen for reading this story and giving me most helpful advice. Many thanks also to Roger and Claire Ash-Wheeler for their hospitality at the Boat House by the River Dart, where I was able to work on the story undisturbed.

—Satish Kumar

CHAPTER ONE

Encountering

the Monster

long time ago in North India,
along the Gangetic plain,
Gautama, the Buddha, came to
Savatthi and found the town deserted: shops locked,
houses closed, and streets empty. The Buddha was
seeking food for his midday meal. He knocked at
the door of a devoted disciple, the Lady Nandini,
who looked out of a window anxiously. Seeing the
Buddha, she hurriedly unlocked the door and urged
him to come inside. As soon as he was in, she bolted
the door again. The Buddha was bemused.

"What's the matter?" the Buddha asked in a
puzzled voice. "I see fear on your face. Why are the
streets empty of people?"

"Don't you know, my lord?" said Nandini.
"A man known as Angulimala has been terrorizing
the town and murdering people."

She took a deep breath. She felt worried that the Buddha, unaware and vulnerable, was going about the town without protection. What would happen if Angulimala met the Buddha? Nandini shivered at the thought.

"Who is Angulimala?" asked the Buddha.

"He wears the necklace (*mala*) of human fingers (*anguli*) and so he has become known as Angulimala. He is merciless. He is murdering men for their fingers. He is strong, skilled and daring—and he is cunning. He has destroyed villages and towns. Everyone is frightened of him."

A profound seriousness appeared on the face of the Buddha. He remained silent and thoughtful.

Nandini gave the Buddha a bowl of rice soaked in mango juice and honey, but her mind was not on food. She was thinking of Angulimala.

"Please stay here," Nandini begged the Buddha. "Do not go out alone, it is dangerous."

"But my disciples wait for me in the Jeta Grove. I must go."

"No, not to the Jeta Grove! In the forest, between here and the Jeta Grove, hides Angulimala. Please do not go, my lord, at least not through that forest. Angulimala will know no difference between the compassionate Buddha and an ordinary mortal. Take no such risk. He is a wanted criminal. There is a reward of a thousand gold coins on his head."

"Nandini, the Buddha has no fear of death, and the Buddha does not change his plans out of fear. The rice soaked in mango juice was truly nourishing. I am satisfied. Thank you for your gracious gift."

The Buddha turned toward the locked door. But Nandini was reluctant to let him go.

"I am waiting for you to unlock the door."

"Please, my lord, please listen. Do not approach Angulimala. He is very dangerous."

"Gracious Nandini, trust the Buddha, he is fully aware of what he is doing. Free yourself from fear."

"But I fear for your life, Illustrious One," said Nandini.

"Life lived in fear is no life," answered the Buddha. "It might be the job of the King to kill the criminals, but the calling of the Buddha is to transform them, awaken them, and liberate them from ignorance. So, Nandini, do not dissuade me from my duty."

"But believe me, my lord, Angulimala is beyond the pale," Nandini pleaded.

"Sweet Nandini, I understand your concerns," replied the Buddha. "But understand that my love, my friendship, and my compassion are not limited to those who are already in agreement with me. I must reach out to those who are possessed with anger and ignorance. Healing the wounded soul is my vocation. I am not worried about my life, or my death—I am worried about Angulimala."

To Nandini, the innocence of the Buddha bordered on naïveté. While she was thinking of ways to dissuade him from confronting Angulimala, she heard his final words:

"Nandini, I am happy to die, if that is what it takes to save Angulimala."

With shaking hands Nandini unlocked the door, yet she was still afraid. She imagined the fingers of the Buddha hanging from Angulimala's neck, and shivered at the thought.

"My lord, be careful, be very careful. Go well."

The Buddha raised his hand in blessing and walked calmly away. Soon he left the town behind.

The Buddha followed the path to the Jeta Grove through the fields alone, unhindered and undisturbed, deep into the cool of the woods. He kept walking, going deeper and deeper into the forest. In the stillness of the trees, the Buddha's steps were the only sound, and the only man to hear them was Angulimala. He wondered, "What is this sound? Who is walking? Who dares to come and invade my territory?"

In the distance he saw a figure in a yellow robe moving slowly. Angulimala shook his head in disbelief, then looked again. The moving figure was coming toward him.

Feeling happy, Angulimala grabbed his sword and stood up.

"Ah ha! I am going to get ten more fingers for my necklace without much effort!" he said to himself.

He brandished his sword and moved toward the approaching figure. Seeing his furious face, the

Buddha realized that he must be Angulimala. The Buddha smiled and kept moving. Angulimala was amazed. He had never encountered a person who was not afraid of him and did not run away from him.

"Doesn't this ignorant fool know who I am? Soon he will know," murmured Angulimala.

Within seconds he heard a sweet voice calling, "Angulimala, Angulimala, Angulimala."

"How puzzling! He obviously knows me, knows my name and yet . . . and yet?"

Angulimala shouted back loudly, "Who are you? Why aren't you running away from me? Don't you know I am going to kill you without blinking an eye and thread your fingers onto my necklace?"

"Yes, yes. I know who you are. But do you know that I can be killed without blinking an eye?" The Buddha paused for a moment, and then said, "I am always ready to die. Dying harms no one. But killing? How do you feel about killing others, Angulimala? Have you looked deeply into your feelings about killing?"

The Buddha looked at the man in front of him. Blood was still dripping from some of the fingers on his necklace. His bloodstained clothes and sweating body gave off a disturbing smell. Aggression emanated from his heavy black mustache and beard and his long matted hair. His strong and fearsome appearance would have driven away most mortals, but the Buddha stood like a rock.

"I know you can kill me, and maybe you will," said the Buddha. "But when you kill, you kill none other than yourself. Because I am none other than you, and you are none other than me. Whatever you do to me you do to yourself, Angulimala.

Let me tell you one thing. You are capable not only of killing. You are also capable of loving, you are capable of compassion. You are capable of change, you are capable of friendship."

The Buddha stopped speaking and smiled.

"I have no friends."

"But I am your friend, Angulimala; that is why I have come to meet you and speak to you."

Angulimala trembled, listening to these words.

"You, my friend? I have given up all friendships. I have abandoned the world."

Buddha was pleased. Angulimala was talking, using his tongue rather than his sword.

"Why have you abandoned the world, Angulimala?"

"Because the world abandoned me."

"Why did the world abandon you?"

"Because my village abandoned me."

"Why did your village abandon you?"

"Because my family abandoned me."

"Why did your family abandon you?"

"Because my mother abandoned me."

"Why did your mother abandon you, Angulimala?"

"Because my mother followed my father; she loved me and yet she abandoned me, because my father abandoned me."

"Why did your father abandon you?" asked the Buddha in a low voice.

"Because I disagreed with him, I disobeyed him, I rebelled against him. I wanted to stand up for myself and follow my own path, but he would not let me. One day I hit him. I was angry with him."

Buddha closed his eyes. He took a deep breath and then spoke in a soothing voice. "Angulimala, were you so overcome with anger that you saw yourself separate from your father? Was this feeling of separation the cause of the quarrel between you and your father? Is it not true, Angulimala, that before you abandoned your father you abandoned your sense of connection? Is it not true then that you are yourself the cause of all abandonment? Angulimala, I am your friend and I want to help you to recognize the cause of your pain and your problems, to recognize your sorrow and suffering, and to recognize that there is no one else responsible for your actions other than yourself."

Angulimala stood speechless. No one had ever confronted him like this.

Angulimala remembered his childhood, one of deprivation. He remembered the days when he was humiliated by the high-caste youngsters; when his father was despised and denounced by men of superior birth. At the time he knew of no other way to deal with his anger than to take it out on his father. But what could his father do? Poor man, he was also a victim of his birth and circumstances. For Angulimala to blame his father and his family was no solution to the conditions of his community. He wished he had met earlier a man like this monk, this Buddha, who was able to listen and guide him out of his lonely battle against himself.

After a few moments of reflection, he said, "I never thought of my life in this way. When I abandoned my home I did so in search of freedom and dignity for myself, for my family, for my people. I met a magician, a dispenser of power which, he said, 'resides on the edge of the sword.' I said to him, 'I want to be powerful, what shall I do?' In response the shaman put a charm on this sword and gave it to me. He promised, 'If you kill one hundred men with this sword, and wear a garland of a thousand fingers, you will be able to impose your will upon others and you will rule the world.' Ever since I have been on a mission to kill, to make myself invincible. Now you come along and tell me something totally different. Are you a shaman?"

"I want you to find power within yourself. That inner power is greater than power over others. You and your people suffer because the king and the caste-ridden society impose power over you. Now you wish to impose your power over others. You have a love of power as strong as that of your enemies. Try the power of love. The power of the self is greater than the power of the sword. The power of love grows from inside, whereas the power of the sword is imposed from the outside. Like a tree grows from a seed, the power of love grows from the self; seek your power within and be your own light."

Angulimala found himself perplexed. He said,

"The power of the sword is immediate and clear. But I know nothing about the power of the self."

The Buddha smiled at Angulimala's apparent confusion. "The power of the sword is dependent on the weakness, submission, and powerlessness of others. The power of love empowers everyone: it is self-organizing and self-sustaining. All beings, human and other than human, are naturally equipped with this intrinsic power, and it is released through the relationship of mutuality, reciprocity, friendship, and love. All efforts of control over and conflict with others end in tears, frustration, disappointment—or war."

"But why should I believe you?" Angulimala interjected. "How do I know that what you say is true?"

"I say this to you, Angulimala, because I have experienced it," replied the Buddha.

"How did you experience it? What makes you so fearless, that you are not afraid of anything, even death, that you are able to come to me knowing that I may kill you? Who are you?"

"I am the awakened one. I am the Buddha."

"From which sleep are you awakened?"

"From the sleep of separation, of ignorance, of anguish, the sleep of wishing to control others, to have power over others. I was born a prince, with plenty of palaces, a thousand horses, a thousand elephants, a thousand soldiers, a thousand servants. I would have been a king. I could have conquered neighboring nations to become an emperor."

"Then what happened?"

"Then one day I went out of my palace. I saw an old man, I saw a sick man, and I saw a dead man, and I realized that in spite of my palaces and my soldiers and my diamonds, I could not escape from sickness, nor from old age, nor from death. So what was the good of all that power and wealth? So, like you, Angulimala, I too abandoned my father, my mother, my wife, my child, my kingdom. But not in anger, not to seek power over others, but to realize the power within, the power of the spirit, the power of love and compassion, the power of friendship," explained the Buddha.

"How can you be a friend of someone who is about to kill you?" protested Angulimala.

"I am the friend of everyone. I am not a prophet, I am not a guru, I am not a saint; I am a friend of all living beings, a friend of all humans irrespective of their qualities, their status, their wealth, their caste. I am a friend of those who are considered to be good, but I am also a friend of those who are condemned as bad. I particularly enjoy being a friend to those who are deprived, excluded, and poor. It is easy to be a friend of the great and the good, but I cherish friendship with those who are labeled as murderers, terrorists, and criminals. I want to console them. They are not bad, they are just asleep, ignorant, and disconnected. Friendship is the way of connecting and waking up."

"But I find it hard to be a friend to those who exercise power over me. I feel angry," Angulimala said.

"That is why I have come to you, Angulimala," said the Buddha. "I want to hold your hand. Will you come with me? I will take you across the river of sorrow and suffering. I will take you to the shore of liberation. I want you to know that your anguish can end; your anger and alienation are not forever. Change is the eternal law of life. Will you embrace transformation? You can have my head and my ten fingers, or you can have all of me and my friendship. The choice is yours. This is the moment of decision."

These challenging words were unbearable. The sword had already dropped from the hand of Angulimala. He began to sob. He could not understand how a high-caste prince could listen to somebody who was born into a low caste, committing the sin of killing every day. Angulimala wondered: "How could this son of a king, a high priest of religion, talk to me and offer friendship to me, when he knows that any association with me can only bring him trouble?"

Full of doubts, Angulimala stood there confused. The Buddha's soothing words of peace, his deep eyes full of promise and longing, shook Angulimala to the core. He was touched by the presence of the Buddha as if under a magic spell. As the hesitant Angulimala stood there in stunned silence, he saw the Buddha turning around and walking away.

When the Buddha started to walk away, Angulimala picked up his sword and followed. His body moved, even though his mind was still uncertain. The Buddha walked faster, and Angulimala was left behind. He increased his pace to catch up with the Buddha, but could not. Then he ran. He thought, "I used to be able to catch a galloping horse or a running deer, but I am now unable to catch up with this monk who appears to be walking at his normal pace. What is the matter with me?"

"Stop, monk, stop," he shouted. "Don't leave me behind."

"I have stopped, Angulimala," the Buddha replied. "I stopped ages ago, but have you? And will you?"

"While you are walking faster than me, you say you have stopped. What do you mean? How have you stopped when you are still moving?"

"I stopped a long time ago," Buddha said. "It is you who have not stopped. I stopped trampling over other people, I stopped desiring to control and dominate people, but you think freedom lies in killing and overpowering others. True stopping is to stop interfering in other people's lives for your own ends. You are rebelling against the oppression of others, but you yourself are oppressive—you are frightening and terrorizing towns and villages. How can terror bring freedom?"

"Human beings do not love each other," Angulimala replied. "The rich are cruel to the poor. The high castes are vicious and deceitful to the lower castes. Why should I love them? I will not stop until I have killed them all."

"Angulimala, I know you have suffered at the hands of the higher caste, the rich and powerful. There is cruelty in the world but cruelty cannot be dissolved by cruelty, oppression cannot be ended by oppression. Fire cannot be put out with more fire. Try to overcome cruelty with compassion, hatred with love, and injustice with forgiveness. Stop traveling on the road of hatred and violence. That is true stopping. Stopping leads to calming,

calming to resting, resting to healing; healing of self as well as healing of others."

The Buddha looked into the eyes of Angulimala and said, "You are deluding yourself if you think that once you have killed one hundred people and taken control of other people's lives you will be happy. Are you happy now?" asked the Buddha.

"No, I am not happy," confessed Angulimala.

"Then how can you predict that you will be happy in the future, when you are sowing the seeds of unhappiness in the present? How can you sow thistles and expect roses? Now is the moment to live fully, and live in happiness. If there is no happiness today, how can you expect to be happy tomorrow? Happiness is born of kindness. When you are kind you are happy, and when you are happy you are kind."

The Buddha's words penetrated deeply into Angulimala's heart. "I have never met a man who

looks, speaks, and smiles like that," he thought.
He realized the futility of his ways, the futility
of killing and violence, the futility of power. He
looked at his predicament, and it was miserable.
He reflected on his past, and it was confused. "If
I reject the help, the advice, and friendship of the
Buddha and go on with my killing spree, what
will I really achieve?" Angulimala asked himself.
It was a moment of reckoning, a moment of self-
realization and enlightenment.

The Buddha looked into Angulimala's eyes as
if he was asking, "Choose, Angulimala, choose!
Either you kill me or surrender to me. The choice
is yours." There was a sudden breakthrough:
Angulimala forced his sword into the ground,
wrenched off the finger necklace, pulled out the
sword from the earth, and with a few quick stabs
dug a hole with its broad blade. Then he pushed
the necklace into the hole and buried it in the soil.

"Here you are. Here you are. Away with the

necklace. Away with the sword. Away with violence. I have stopped."

The Buddha watched Angulimala's actions in amazement. He had seen many warriors, noblemen, courtesans, queens, and kings undergo a change of heart, but never before had he witnessed such rapid transformation.

"I see, Angulimala, I see. Now you have stopped," the Buddha smiled. With his necklace, Angulimala had also left behind his anger, like a snake shedding its old skin.

Then they walked together in utter silence through the peaceful forest. Birds were singing and angels were smiling. The pair came to a pond filled with lotus flowers. Buddha stood still and picked one lotus and held it up in front of Angulimala.

"Look at it—look at this lotus. Its roots are deep in the mud, but the flower is always above the water. However much rain falls, the lotus shakes it off. The lotus is soft, gentle, pleasing, beautiful, and friendly. We too can be like a lotus if we embrace its qualities."

Angulimala took hold of Buddha's left hand and pressed it firmly. This was a sign and Buddha understood it. Angulimala had decided to follow the Buddha all the way to the Jeta Grove.

"Angulimala, as you were the cause of your suffering, you are also the key to your happiness, your source of joy. Inner power gives you peace which is enduring. I can see peace in your eyes, Angulimala. I have seen many people change and transform, but you are very special. Transformation has happened to you instantly."

"The moment I saw you, I felt a connection with you," said Angulimala, "and now I see myself connected with the whole universe."

Ananda, one of the leading disciples of the Buddha, trembled to see the wild man striding along beside the Blessed One into the Jeta Grove. He looked in horror at the bloodstained clothes and recoiled at the stench. He couldn't believe his ears when the Buddha announced, "We have a new friend, Ahimsaka ('The Nonviolent One'). He is our new resident at Jeta Grove. Please give him a robe and a bowl, and give him training in the ways of a monk. Please do all you can to make him welcome and comfortable."

Ahimsaka was quick to learn. Soon he was assimilated into the community. Within a few days he was totally at ease in the life of Jeta Grove, like a fish in a pond. Not only was he himself able to understand the teachings of the Buddha, but he could explain them to others in a lucid and clear way.

CHAPTER TWO

The Conversion

of a King

For King Pasenadi of Savatthi and his army, the terrorist Angulimala was still on the loose, hiding in the forest, always elusive, always on the run. They had been searching for him for many weeks and were frustrated by the failure of their efforts. The King had announced that he himself would lead the hunt and leave no stone unturned, no cave unsearched, no valley unexplored. Sooner or later he would capture Angulimala, dead or alive.

Together with five hundred elite soldiers mounted on horseback, the King started the search for Angulimala, determined to find and execute this enemy of civilization. They stopped near Jeta Grove, where the Buddha and his monks were camping in bamboo huts. Having learned of the presence of the Buddha, the King halted his soldiers and sent on a messenger to say that he wished to pay his respects to the Illustrious One in person. The Buddha sent back his invitation, and the King entered Jeta Grove on foot.

The Buddha came out of his hut to greet the King.

"Welcome, your Majesty. What an unexpected pleasure."

The King and the Buddha walked together to a nearby mango tree and sat down on the bench that was the Buddha's usual place to receive visitors.

The Buddha asked, "Is there something wrong, great King? Has an enemy state attacked your kingdom? Or have some other hostile forces invaded your state? It is unusual to see you in battle dress, accompanied by so many horsemen."

The King replied, "No—no one has attacked

us, but there is an enemy within. There is an evil man on the run who is terrorizing travelers, ambushing unwary innocent people and killing them indiscriminately. I have come to warn you, Enlightened One, that this area is not a safe place for you and your monks. May I leave some of my soldiers to protect Jeta Grove? Your security is my prime concern."

Buddha knew whom the King was talking about, and yet he asked, "Who is this person who gives you so much trouble and disturbs your peace?"

"He is known as Angulimala—a monstrous madman, a butcher, a hater of human beings. We are out to find him. But in the meantime we must protect the people."

The Buddha had no alternative but to find a way to tell the King that he need not bother to search for Angulimala.

"Your Majesty, if I were to tell you that

Angulimala has given up his campaign of violence, would you believe me?"

"No, I could not believe it. You don't know the viciousness of this wicked man. He can never change. The only solution is to capture and execute him."

The Buddha fell silent, and thought of how to break the news of Angulimala's conversion. After a moment's reflection the Buddha said, "Your Majesty, everything changes; we are all capable of change. Not only are we capable of change—change is inevitable. There is only one thing which does not change, and that is 'change' itself."

"What are you talking about? These fine principles of philosophy are all very well, but we are dealing here with a confirmed criminal. The only change we can expect in this case is that Angulimala will change from bad to worse. There is no hope whatsoever that Angulimala can give up his evil actions."

"Your Majesty, if I were to tell you that in reality Angulimala has become a monk and has taken refuge in me, in my community and in my teachings, then what? If I were to tell you he has shaved his head, taken a bowl and a robe and renounced all violence, then what? If I were to tell you that Angulimala has resolved not to harm a fly, even a mosquito, never mind a man or woman, then what?"

"This is something beyond my imagination, Enlightened One," said the King. "I am unable to comprehend what you speak about. Do you have any evidence to prove it?"

"Your Majesty, before I offer you evidence, I want to ask you one question. If what I say is found to be true, will you pardon Angulimala?"

"Enlightened One, I am a king. My duty is to

uphold justice and impose punishment on those who have committed crimes. How can I pardon Angulimala when fathers and mothers, brothers and wives of those whom Angulimala has killed are crying out for justice?"

"Your Majesty, violence breeds violence. Revenge and justice are not the same. Someone, somewhere, needs to take courage to break the cycle of violence. Forgiveness is superior to justice. Being kind and compassionate to those who are good to you is easy. True forgiveness and compassion come only when one is able to forgive even those who have committed barbaric acts. If Angulimala is capable of renouncing violence, then tell me, your Majesty: is your civilized society also capable of being truly civilized and renouncing violence?"

The King was speechless. He had never been challenged like this before. The choice between justice and compassion was a hard one. He sat there, gazing at the Buddha.

After a few still moments the Buddha stood up.

"Let us take a short walk, your Majesty."

As they walked together the King repeated, "Angulimala is an evil man through and through. Make no mistake. Even if he pretends to change, I do not believe that he really can."

There was desperation in the voice of the King.

"Evil is born from ignorance, your Majesty. When ignorance is dispelled, we are enlightened."

The Buddha and the King walked to the pond filled with beautiful lotus flowers. The Buddha picked a lotus and held it between himself and the King and said, "Your Majesty, the lotus has no enemies, the lotus has no anger, the lotus knows not whom to please or whom to offend, the lotus judges not. The lotus gives pleasure to saints and sinners alike. Why can't humans be like a lotus? Angulimala killed people because he was filled with anger. You too are filled with anger and wish to kill him. How can anyone dissolve anger with more anger? Fire cannot be extinguished by adding more fuel—only water can extinguish fire. Only with love can we overcome hate. Only with trust can we overcome fear."

The Buddha offered the lotus to the King and took hold of his hand. They continued to walk.

After a few steps they came to another tree, under which there was a bamboo platform. A monk was speaking in a serene voice, teasing a group of people. The Buddha and the King stopped, and stood nearby listening:

"There are Four Noble Truths: suffering, sorrow, pain, problems, difficulties—these are part of life. There is no good denying them. There is no good running away from them. This is the first truth. But all problems and pain have a cause, and when we go deep enough we will realize that we ourselves are causing suffering by our ignorance, by our ego, by our attachment, by our clinging to our desires, and by our conditioning. This is the second truth. But there is no need to be despondent and to give up hope. Things change: what begins comes to an end; suffering can end; problems can be solved. We can learn to let go of our attachments, to be more accepting of life as it is. In this way our problems and suffering can be dissolved. This is the third truth. We are not merely victims of our fate, we can be active participants in the process of life. There are ways which can help us to overcome sorrow and end suffering. This is the fourth noble truth."

Listening to these words, the King was impressed and inspired.

"Who is this new monk of such profound insight and understanding?" he asked. "I have never seen him before. He explains the Four Noble Truths in such a simple and clear way. I wish he could teach this wisdom to everyone in my kingdom."

Yes, your Majesty, but please consider the following: his name is Ahimsaka, the Nonviolent One. Previously he was known as Angulimala—the same Angulimala whom you seek to punish."

The King was shocked and alarmed. His hair stood on end. He felt giddy, he fainted and fell to the ground sweating. The Buddha knelt down and fanned him with a corner of his robe. Suddenly Ahimsaka noticed that someone had collapsed; he stopped his teaching, ran to the pond, and brought a bowl of water. He tore off a piece from his robe, wet it, and placed it on the forehead of the King. Then he rubbed the King's feet to stimulate the circulation. A few minutes later the King regained consciousness and sat up facing Ahimsaka. Their eyes met and communicated something without words. Compassion overcame the King.

"Thank you, Ahimsaka, for your caring. You have healing hands. I am moved by your teachings.

I did not believe the Buddha when he spoke about you. Now I am convinced that you are completely transformed. But please do not leave Jeta Grove. You will not be safe outside this sanctuary."

"Your Majesty, I have done much harm to your people. I have brought anguish and loss. I have deprived them of their loved ones. So it is my noble duty to undertake the work of healing and to remove the seeds of discord. I must overcome fear and come to Savatthi. I must confront my past, and face the future."

CHAPTER THREE

❊

Freedom
from Fear

few days later, Ahimsaka entered the bamboo hut of the Buddha who was sitting in the lotus position meditating on his breathing. Ahimsaka sat down to one side and watched the Buddha taking deep breaths.

When Ahimsaka saw that the Buddha had noticed him, he asked, "O Enlightened One, may I have your permission to go to Savatthi and seek forgiveness of those whose lives I have harmed? May I go and beg for food and communicate some of what I have learned from you to the citizens of Savatthi?"

"Yes, my beloved Ahimsaka, yes. You may go and seek alms, but only once in twenty-four hours; and if someone offers you two pieces of bread, take only one. Meet your needs by taking food from more than one house, so that no one feels burdened by giving to a monk. Beg like a honeybee which goes from flower to flower, taking only a little nectar from each. Never has a flower complained of a honeybee harming it. Such should be the way of a begging monk."

"Yes, Enlightened One. I will follow the way of the honeybee. But some people are bound to recognize me and they may abuse me and swear at me. Please, Buddha, guide me. How should I respond?"

"Say to yourself that people are kind, they are only abusing you verbally; at least they are not hitting you. For that, be thankful."

"But some people may be so angry that they may hit me. What then should I do?"

"Ahimsaka, it will be hard for you, but keep calm and think that they are only hitting you and not throwing stones at you."

"It is possible that some of them will throw stones at me. What then should I do?"

"That will be a harder test for you, but even then, think that although they are throwing stones at you, at least they are not punching or kicking you."

"But I can imagine that some will even kick and punch me until I fall to the ground bleeding."

"Then, Ahimsaka, remember my teaching of endurance, and say to yourself that although you are hurt, wounded, and bleeding, they have not killed you."

"Thank you, my lord, but if they kill me?"

"Ahimsaka, you will not know that you are killed. Everyone who is born will one day die. When you are dying, if you are still conscious then think that you are being liberated from this body and from all the memories which burden your mind. Death is a door to liberation. Be thankful for it."

"Your teachings give me courage. I am free from the fear of death. May I leave on my journey to Savatthi?"

"Yes, Ahimsaka, you may leave. If you are in the east street of the town, look out for a large thatched house with a blue door. There is a well in front of the house and a *sal* tree. This is the house of Nandini, a friend and follower of the Buddha. You may seek alms from her, and please convey my blessings to her."

Ahimsaka was in Savatthi. The town was beginning to emerge from the shock of so many murders. During the past few weeks, all had been quiet: no new killings had been committed by Angulimala. Even the police had relaxed their vigil. Rumors had been circulating that Angulimala had been eaten by a lion in the forest, or that he had become an ascetic, or that the King had captured him and he was being held secretly in a dungeon. Nobody knew for sure what had happened to Angulimala.

Ahimsaka stood outside the house of Nandini under the *sal* tree. He saw the door locked, and decided to wait so that he could convey the greetings of the Buddha to her.

"So good to see a monk in town—things must be returning to normal," said a stranger.

"These followers of the Buddha believe in nonviolence. But how can you be nonviolent when faced with a murderer?" commented another man.

The monk listened to these words with equanimity.

Another man spoke up. "Nonviolence is all very well until you are confronted with diehard criminals who are determined to destroy the good order of society. The only way to deal with such people is to hang them!" This angry voice penetrated the ears of monk Ahimsaka, but he continued to listen.

A few men and women started to gather around the waiting monk, who stood in silence.

"Who are you?" a child asked.

"I am a disciple of Lord Buddha, the Enlightened One, who is showing the path of compassion and who at present resides in the Jeta Grove."

More people gathered. "No one can have compassion for a terrorist like Angulimala," someone yelled from the crowd.

"The Buddha has compassion for all. He teaches unconditional love."

"How can you love an evil man?" shouted another person.

"My Lord the Buddha teaches that good and evil pass through every human heart, and good is more powerful than evil. He teaches that we should overcome evil with good."

As the monk spoke, someone shouted, "This man is not only a sympathizer but resembles

Angulimala. I have seen the killer. Could it be that Angulimala is hiding in a monk's robe?"

"Yes, you are right. This monk certainly resembles Angulimala."

"Who are you? You must be the murderer! Tell us the truth!" People accused him.

The monk quietly spoke. "In the past, I was filled with anger. I killed people and wore their fingers as my necklace. Then I met the Buddha; he opened my eyes and changed my heart. I took refuge in him."

"You deceive us! You are a cheat, a sinner, an evil man, a murderer, a robber, a terrorist. You must be punished. You must be hanged."

"You killed my brother," shouted one.

"You killed my son," cried another.

"You killed my husband," said a woman.

"You must face the consequences of your deeds," many voices roared together.

A tall man struck Ahimsaka's face. Another blow followed. An old man hit him on the head with a stick. A boy threw a stone. Someone else punched him in the stomach. Another kicked him so hard that he fell to the ground. The monk had a black eye and many bruises and had started to bleed.

Returning home, Nandini found her way blocked by the rioting crowd. Her groom forced the carriage through to where the monk in a saffron robe lay on the ground, bleeding. Shocked and surprised, Nandini challenged the mob, "Stop, stop! How can you be so cruel? This monk is a follower of my beloved Lord Buddha. He wears his robe."

Nandini threw her shawl over the monk and put her own body between the monk and the angry crowd. Her driver helped to lift the monk into the carriage.

"He is a murderer! He is a killer! He is Angulimala!" people shouted.

"If he was Angulimala, he would be killing you and me. Why would Angulimala stand and take blows from you? Why would Angulimala have a bowl and a robe? You are mistaken," Nandini shouted back as they drove away.

The monk was still conscious but in pain. Nandini put a bandage round his bleeding head.

"Let me take you to your hermitage, monk. Where do you come from?"

"I live in the Jeta Grove with the Buddha himself, who sends you his greetings. Aren't you Nandini?"

"I am. And I am a devotee of the wise Buddha. His guidance and his love have saved my life."

"O noble Nandini, Buddha has praised you. He loves you too."

"Quick, charioteer—drive fast so we can attend to the monk's wounds before it is too late."

CHAPTER FOUR

Spiritual

Simplicity

he Buddha saw Nandini's carriage arrive at speed. Soon he realized that Ahimsaka had been attacked. He asked Ananda to bring an infusion of neem leaves and water, and to pick potent fresh wild herbs from the forest for poultices. As Ananda hurried to prepare the treatment, the Buddha welcomed Nandini and offered his shoulder to Ahimsaka to step down from the carriage. Nandini too gave a hand to support Ahimsaka. As he limped along he said, "I am all right, I am all right."

The Buddha and Nandini brought him to his hut. Ananda with fellow monks began to nurse him. Exhausted, Ahimsaka relaxed and fell asleep.

"Let him rest now," whispered the Buddha. "Sleep is the best treatment. One of you should keep constant watch by his hut, in case he wakes."

The Buddha was filled with joy to see Nandini and was grateful that she had brought Ahimsaka home. They walked together to the platform under the mango tree and sat down.

"Is he really Angulimala? Or are the people in Savatthi confused and mistaken? He is so pious and gentle!"

The Buddha narrated his encounter with Angulimala and the way he transformed into Ahimsaka. He also told her of the visit of King Pasenadi. Nandini was astonished. It was difficult for her to believe all this. Was she dreaming? Could this all be true?

"Your powers of persuasion are truly great, Enlightened One. If it is possible for Angulimala to be transformed in this way, then there is hope for everyone."

"Yes, Nandini, that is why until all living beings are liberated, I will keep coming to the world. I will return as Maitreya, as a friend: not as a prophet, not as a master or guide, not even as a teacher, but simply as a friend. I speak to you as your friend. All beings are Bodhisattvas, potential Buddhas, capable of enlightenment."

Nandini did not feel convinced that she herself was a potential Buddha, but she very much liked the idea of the Buddha as her friend. Although everyone revered him as a great guru, an enlightened master, an illustrious incarnation, and so on, these high-sounding attributes created a barrier of formality and a sense of distance; they produced hierarchy and expectation. So when the Buddha presented himself as a friend, it put Nandini at her ease, and she felt encouraged to seek some very personal advice. She said, "I try to follow your teachings on meditation, but find it hard to focus. It is difficult to be detached from desires, from likes and dislikes, from attractions and aversions. My mind keeps jumping around like a monkey. Tell me, my friend, should I be putting great effort into concentrating the mind or just let it wander?"

"Neither, Nandini," said the Buddha. "You are a musician, you play sitar. How do you tune it?"

"I tune it carefully so the strings are neither too loose nor too tight. Only then will the sitar sound sweet."

"So it is with the mind, Nandini. Allow it to be in balance. Avoid extremes: the middle way is better. Neither force the mind too hard into concentration nor let it wander aimlessly. Meditation is to pay attention, to be aware of your breathing, your posture, your feelings, your perceptions, your thoughts and all that passes through your mind and the mind itself; whatever is going on within you and between you and the universe. Meditation is not just sitting for an hour here or an hour there; meditation is a way of life. It is practiced all the time. There is no separation between meditation and everyday living. When you have ceased to be bound by the past or by the future, when you are fully present in the here and now, then it is meditation."

"This all sounds so simple, Enlightened One, but my memories, my dreams, my doubts, my anxieties dominate me. I wonder whether there is any purpose to this life, I wonder if the universe has a purpose—or does everything exist by chance? I even wonder whether the world was created—or is it without beginning? I wonder whether the world will come to an end—or will it continue for ever? I wonder and wonder constantly, and so I find it impossible to live in the present moment."

In the tranquil surroundings of the Jeta Grove, Nandini was pouring out her problems. She was pleased to find the Buddha on his own, at peace, giving total attention to her. He smiled at Nandini and said, "All your wonderings are metaphysical speculations. What does it matter if the world had a beginning or not? Whether it will last for eternity or come to an end tomorrow? If an arrow hit your driver, would you ask who shot this arrow? Where it came from? In which foundry was it made? Who was the maker? Whether the arrowhead was made of iron or copper? Would you waste your time deliberating on these intellectual questions, or would you focus on pulling out the arrow from the body of the driver and find ways of healing the wound?"

"I would certainly be quick to remove the arrow."

"Then, noble Nandini, why are you wasting your time in pondering irrelevant metaphysical questions when you and your fellow beings are afflicted by suffering that is caused by ego and attachment? Isn't it urgent to look at your suffering, the origin of suffering, the cessation of suffering, and the ways to end suffering?"

Buddha was speaking with clarity. Nandini could feel the force of his convictions, but her intellect was resisting.

"Nevertheless, I want to find the truth," said Nandini, "the truth about the arrow. How can I rest without knowing the truth? It is essential to find the truth and establish facts."

"Truth is only one virtue among many, and it is an elusive virtue at that," explained the Buddha. "Truth has to sit within the family of virtues. Seeking truth is not enough—especially not at the expense of addressing the pain of the present moment. Seeking compassion, love, generosity, friendship, and happiness is important too. Moreover, these virtues are more helpful in ending suffering than the pursuit of truth."

"I do see your point," nodded Nandini, "but the problems of everyday life are not that simple."

After a brief pause she said, "I believe you to be a wise man, so I will try to follow your teachings."

But the Buddha wished to take no such responsibility. He said, "Nandini, don't just follow me. Don't just accept this because I say so: try it for yourself, test it in your life. If you find that what I say resonates with your experience and with your own truth, only then accept it. If I tell you about the sweetness, the softness, and the fragrance of a mango fruit, it won't mean much. When you try it, taste it, and experience it for yourself, only then will you know what a mango is. Wisdom cannot be communicated in words or concepts or theories; it has to be discovered and experienced by yourself. My teaching to you is like pointing a finger to the moon. My finger is not the moon. Forget my finger and look at the moon. I say this to you because I have direct knowledge of suffering and

I have direct knowledge of the end of suffering through the Noble Eightfold Path. This Eightfold Path of right view, right intention, right speech, right action, right livelihood, right effort, right mindfulness, and right concentration leads to peace, harmony, wholeness, and enlightenment."

"You speak of right view and right action, but how is one to know what is right and what is wrong?" asked Nandini.

"Whatever lessens suffering in yourself and others, that is right. Whatever increases suffering, that is wrong. The answer is within you. When you are free of pride and prejudice, when you are calm and attentive, a light will shine within you. Through meditation and through being mindful you will find your own knowledge of rightness. You will be your own light. Just be true to yourself Nandini, just be yourself."

After a few moments, the Buddha continued,

"I can point out the moon, but you will have to see the moon with your own eyes, and you will see it when you look up."

There was nothing more for Nandini to argue with. The Buddha had given her profound insights: much to meditate upon, and to practice.

Nandini took a walk to the lotus pond, and while she reflected upon the simple and restrained lifestyle of the Buddha, a deep sense of despondency overwhelmed her like a dark cloud. "The Buddha has only three robes," she thought. "One for the day, one for the night, and one to change into after bathing. His robes are a patchwork of many pieces of old cloth sewn together. He has just one blanket to sleep on and just one bowl for his food. He eats only once a day. Is he the same Siddhartha, who was the prince of many possessions? Now he is practicing utter restraint, whereas here I am possessed by my possessions. My life is cluttered with so many objects—no wonder that my mind is cluttered. The Enlightened One is the master of his life, and therefore he is the master of the world. I am a mere manager of my goods and chattels. And yet I love my creature comforts—my saris of silk, my shawls of soft wool, my soft bed, my saffron rice, my servants, and my groom—I can't imagine shaving my head and possessing only three robes. How can I reconcile my longing for liberation and my attachment to the world? I am comfortable, but I am not happy. I want to be happy as well as comfortable. The Buddha doesn't seem to be bothered, but I am."

Once again many doubts descended upon her. Sad and perplexed, Nandini sat by the pond holding her head in her hands.

The Buddha saw her from a distance. He realized that all was not well with Nandini, so he walked slowly down to the pond.

"Has the Buddha's discourse disturbed you, Nandini? You look worried."

"I am infected by doubts and dilemmas. You live a life of great restraint. You are happy with so little, but this is beyond me."

"Nandini, do not be so concerned with external forms, with appearances. You can practice loving-kindness wherever you are. What you consider the frugality and simplicity of our life in Jeta Grove is not imposed or contrived; it arises naturally. Simplicity of material possessions is only one aspect of spiritual practice; what is more important is to simplify your inner life. Empty yourself of ambitions, likes, and dislikes." The Buddha spoke in a consoling voice.

"What do you mean by inner simplicity?" asked Nandini.

"More than our external burdens, we are burdened by the internal confusion of identity. Be free of such confusion, Nandini. Be empty of the idea of a separate self, a separate I. What does 'I' consist of? Am I my legs or my arms? Am I my intellect or my feelings? Am I my perceptions? Am I Siddhartha, a prince born in the Sakya clan? Who am I? What is my identity? I am no one thing. I am everything. I am not an isolated, autonomous, separate self. There is nothing to hold on to. Nothing to be attached to. I am a microcosm of the macrocosm. I am the universe itself. Life is a flow of energy: it takes a form and then dissolves. All forms are waves on the surface of the sea of life. They rise and they fall; there is no point in being attached to a changing form. Be the wave, and know that you are part of the great ocean of existence. That is the ultimate simplicity."

"But I am Nandini. I am this body, this flesh and blood." She touched her face with both hands, and said, "I am this person with my own individual personality, with my own soul."

"You are and you are not. If you look beyond,

you will see the big picture. What is left of you if the food you eat, the water you drink, the air you breathe is taken away from your body? What you call your 'individual personality' or your particular soul did not drop from the sky. Take away your father and your mother, take away all the ancestral influences you have inherited, take away all the culture, language, and perceptions you have acquired: then what will be left of you? In this big picture, you carry within you the entire history of evolution as well as millions of years of the future to come, the entire network of relationships, the continuous dance of life; you are much much more than this small individual soul imprisoned in this flesh and blood personality. You are infinitely flowing energy, you are indivisible; and that is what makes you individual."

"I see," said Nandini. "I seem to have got into the habit of clinging to my separate self, but now

I understand that the entire existence including myself is a dance of energy which moves without boundaries: from earth to humans and back to the earth and everything in between."

"Exactly so, Nandini," said the Buddha. "All life and everything besides flow into each other."

Nandini bowed to the Buddha. She felt calmer, and made her way home.

CHAPTER FIVE

Seeking

Revenge

While the wounded Ahimsaka rested in his hut at Jeta Grove, the crowd in Savatthi was still busy arguing.

"We should have killed him," shouted one.

"He's only pretending to be a monk," said another.

"No, no, we cannot take the law into our own hands, so let us go to the King. Let's inform him that we have found Angulimala and demand that he should be arrested."

"Who will get the reward?"

"I was the first to recognize him," said a young man.

"No, no, you weren't. It was I who spotted him," claimed another.

"Look, how many are we here? One, two,

three . . . ten. We all found him together; let us share the reward among ourselves—one hundred gold coins each."

They were pleased with the prospect of becoming wealthy.

Fortunately for them, they arrived at the court at the time of the public audience, when the King heard the concerns of ordinary citizens.

"Your Majesty, we have some good news. We have found the most wanted terrorist, criminal number one, the enemy of the people, Angulimala. He is disguised as a monk and living with the Buddha in the Jeta Grove. We can identify him."

The King listened patiently and asked, "Where did you see him?"

"Your Majesty, he came to our town. We found him outside the house of the Lady Nandini. She has given him protection and taken him back to the Buddha."

"How do you know that the monk was Angulimala?"

"Your Majesty, we recognized him and he admitted to it, but claims that he has changed and taken refuge in Buddha. But your Majesty, no one can trust Angulimala. As a leopard cannot change its spots, Angulimala cannot change his nature. He is a terrorist through and through. He must be hanged in public and made an example for other terrorists. And, your Majesty, we are flabbergasted that the Lady Nandini and the Buddha are harboring a terrorist. This must not be allowed. Either they are with us or they are against us. If they are giving refuge to a terrorist, then they should also be punished."

"Citizens, please sit down and let us talk. Let me send for a cool drink of mango juice."

"Sir, thank you, but we would like to receive the reward of one thousand gold coins as announced."

"Yes, citizens, you deserve your reward, and

you will have it. But let me tell you this, the Lord Buddha is the most respected, the most wise, and the most enlightened being known to me. If someone takes refuge in him and the Lord Buddha gives him sanctuary in his monastery, then we should honor the rights of a refugee. Would you not agree?"

"No, your Majesty, we cannot agree. With this example other criminals will seek the soft option of taking refuge in Buddha and will escape punishment. Angulimala has devastated our families. We want justice."

"Citizens, we cannot bring your beloved ones back to life by killing Angulimala. Isn't it better to encourage all evildoers to surrender themselves and renounce their evil deeds? If the Buddha is more effective than my armed forces, then why not give him the chance of changing human hearts and persuading criminals to mend their ways?"

"We have never heard such weak words from your Majesty before. We have never seen your

Majesty being so soft. Our nation should never be a sanctuary for criminals."

"Citizens, this is the first time I have come across a terrorist who sees the error of his ways and actually renounces crime. You know, I was out with my five hundred mounted soldiers seeking him, and by chance I happened to be near the sanctuary of the Buddha. To my astonishment I saw Angulimala, heard his teachings, and found him to be born again. As Angulimala changed from being a terrorist to a monk, I changed from being a giver of harsh punishments to a compassionate King. Yes, my citizens, I have seen a new light. I have changed. I have realized that the so-called 'soft option' is the hardest option. It would be easy to declare the Buddha an accomplice and not only to arrest Angulimala but also to arrest the Buddha himself—accusing him of being a protector of terrorists, of aiding and abetting terrorism. That would be easy. Neither the Buddha nor Angulimala have any defenses, whereas my army is well equipped—the strongest and most powerful. Yet now I see the world differently. I see that we need more Buddhas and more monks rather than more soldiers, more police, more prisons."

The citizens heard the King in disbelief. There was a stunned silence. After a while the whispering began. Then they all spoke to each other.

"His Majesty has a point."

"This is a novel method of dealing with criminals."

"What about justice?" said one whose son was killed by Angulimala.

"What about revenge and retribution?" said another, who had lost his brother.

"But where will revenge take us?" asked an old man.

"What about protecting citizens from danger?" questioned a merchant.

"But he is under the supervision of the Buddha

and he has to obey the monastic rules. It is unlikely he will endanger anyone," said a temple priest. "Between the Buddha and his Majesty they must know what is good and what is bad, what is wrong and what is right. We must trust them."

The King observed some signs of satisfaction among his citizens, and called for his treasurer to offer the thousand gold coins to them.

"Citizens, as we now know the whereabouts of Angulimala, it is right and proper that the situation be resolved in public. He should be brought to the court, and due process of justice should be followed. So please go and inform all families whose loved ones have been lost that on the day of the full moon we will gather and deliberate on the case and on future action. We will invite the Buddha and Angulimala, as well as other sages and citizens of the state," commanded the King.

CHAPTER SIX

The Triumph
of Forgiveness

O n the day of the full moon, noble men and women, Brahmin priests, sages from the forests, saddhus in saffron, merchants, and landlords all gathered in the great court of the King. The Buddha himself, accompanied by Ahimsaka and other monks, joined the gathering. Mahavira, the Jina,* with his ascetic followers, also graced the occasion. Even the family of Ahimsaka, his father and mother, brothers, sisters, aunts, uncles, nephews, and nieces together with hundreds of outcaste manual laborers (sudras), poor but dignified, were present, segregated from the rest but within the sight of the King, outside the main Court.

---

*The founder of the Jain religion

Rosewater was sprinkled on the guests, which created a sweet fragrance and calm atmosphere.

"My beloved citizens of Savatthi, this is a difficult day, a day when hurts and wounds inflicted upon many of you are to be recognized and ways found for their healing. Those of you who have been affected and who wish to express their hurt, loss, and suffering are invited to speak openly and without fear."

The King became silent, and a hush fell on the assembly. After some moments, a man stood up from the crowd and spoke:

"One afternoon, my only son, aged thirty, went to visit his friends in a nearby town and never returned. The whole family waited and waited until late at night. Next morning I went to the town and learned from his friends that he had left them early in the evening to return home. 'What happened to him, where is he?' I wondered anxiously. After a long search we found his body thrown in a ditch, all his fingers cut off. The body was lying in a pool of blood. This was the act of Angulimala: he deprived me of my son and heir, without whom my family's future is bleak."

The man was in tears; he could speak no more. The angry audience looked at Angulimala in horror.

A young man quickly got up and said, "I speak for myself and for my grandmother. My grandfather was a blind man and frail, incapable of defending himself. One day he went out for an early morning stroll just to exercise himself, but he was caught by this brutal, cruel Angulimala and struck down in the street and left bleeding to death."

Then a boy stood up and said, "My father went to the forest to collect wood, but he never returned. After many days we found his body with vultures tearing at his flesh. Now I get nightmares about it."

Similar voices of anguish, one after another, continued to shock the gathering, until a thick air of grief depressed the entire court.

The Buddha looked at Ahimsaka and put his hand on his shoulder. All eyes were on him. Breathing in, breathing out deeply, Ahimsaka gathered his courage and composure, he stood up and spoke thus:

"I am guilty of everything that has been said, and much more. You may not think that I deserve forgiveness, and you may be absolutely right. I will accept any verdict declared by the King, who represents the concerns of the entire assembly. If I may be permitted to tell my story, I would be grateful."

Ahimsaka looked at the King.

"Go ahead, go ahead."

"I was born a *dom*, whose duty it is to pick up the bodies of dead animals and deal with them, particularly after the priests have made sacrifice at the altars of the gods. In addition my family and the people of my caste clear the night soil, which is the lowest of the low jobs in our society. My family and other members of my caste are despised, downtrodden, and segregated. The *doms* are considered too dirty to till the land, too dirty to draw water from the public wells, too dirty to touch other people, too dirty to be allowed into the temple, too dirty to hear the holy scriptures, too dirty for others to speak to them. It is as if my family and their caste do not exist.

"As a young man I resented this treatment. I was furious. My father, you out there, tried to calm me down, but that made me even more angry. I rebelled against you. I even hit you, and for that I am sorry."

Ahimsaka took a moment's breath. Everyone was listening in total silence.

"Frustrated and depressed, I left home and came to the conclusion that I must take control of society, be the ruler myself, and bring an end to the oppression and segregation which were destroying me and my people. I sought power through the sword, which brought much anguish and unhappiness to myself and fueled the antagonism between me and society. But now I have seen the light. Thanks to Gautama, the Buddha, I realize that the end cannot justify the means; action should be good and right in the beginning, in the middle, and in the end. Only through a change of heart, a change of consciousness, can we bring an end to oppression. To bring freedom to others, we have to be free within ourselves. So here I am. I await your judgment."

Even though the words of Angulimala were sincere, most people did not see any connection between the caste system and his atrocious actions. They could not see why Angulimala should blame the caste system, or make it an excuse for his crimes. After all, most *doms* and untouchables are law-abiding.

◎ ⊙ ◉

Then Mahavira, the Jina, spoke, "Your Majesty, enlightened Gautama, and citizens. We must realize that violence is not confined to physical violence. Fear is violence, caste discrimination is violence, exploitation of others, however subtle, is violence, segregation is violence, thinking ill of others and condemning others are violence. In order to reduce individual acts of physical violence we must reduce psychological and social violence. We must reform institutions which support violence, we must work to eliminate violence at all levels, mental, verbal, personal, and social, including violence to animals, plants, and all other forms of life. Angulimala's violence was only a fraction of the world of violence, even though it was extreme and obvious, but that violence was connected to the not-so-visible violence which infects our society. Therefore we should thank Angulimala for challenging us to look deeply and examine ourselves."

Suddenly there was uproar. The radical thoughts of Mahavira proved to be too uncomfortable and unpalatable. The crowd could not bear it.

"The caste system and social hierarchy are part of the natural order. This law has been given to us by the ancient sages. It maintains cohesion. We are not gathered here to upset our traditions and dismantle society. We are here to judge the crimes of Angulimala, " protested a Brahmin priest.

There were more and more noises—a general hubbub arose.

"Order! Order!" the King's marshals shouted.

When people fell silent, Mahavira, the Jina, continued. "I know I have raised some fundamental questions, but we must ask the right questions, however uncomfortable they may be, in order to get the right answers. We need to look at the root causes of violence. Otherwise, although we may execute one Angulimala today, there will be many more Angulimalas tomorrow. All humans are born as humans, neither low nor high. Humans must be judged by their acts and not by their birth; by their character and not by their caste. Also we should not forget that animals wish to live, in the same way as humans do. Therefore it is the duty of all good people to respect animals, and not kill them for meat or for ritual."

The people began murmuring uneasily again.

Then Gautama, the Buddha spoke:

"Your Majesty, enlightened Mahavira, and my beloved citizens, it is most kind of our gracious King to invite us here today. We are faced with some vital questions and we are not afraid to seek right answers. We are all changing all the time. The only thing we cannot do is to stop the process of change. Only through change do we grow and evolve, so let us not be afraid of change. Enlightened Mahavira has given us profound words of wisdom. Even if everybody is not able to reach such a high state of nonviolence, we can begin to cultivate small acts of compassion right now. There is a middle way, and the middle way is to use skillful means to refine and reform personal and social relationships. This can be achieved by focusing on the universal truth of interdependence. We are all connected: rich and poor, high caste and low caste, humans and animals. The universe is an interlinked process of unfolding; only through clarity of view and generosity of spirit can we resolve this and all other conflicts."

After the powerful voices of Mahavira and the Buddha, the assembled citizens fell numb and silent. Then the Law Officer of the State rose from his seat and addressed the King.

"Your Majesty, these two great saints of our time have renounced the world, so it is easy for them to speak of nonviolence, compassion, and forgiveness. But we live in the real world. We have heard the anguish of the victims and how their lives have been ruined. If we set Angulimala free, we will be guilty of damaging the social order. Only by giving appropriate punishment to Angulimala can we hope to deter others from becoming criminals. The affairs of state cannot be run purely according to religious rules. The state must impose the rule of law, and therefore, your Majesty, Angulimala must be hanged. Nothing less will do, Sir. The enforcement of the law is paramount."

The Law Officer gained some applause, and then once again a hush descended. King Pasenadi's face appeared anxious, disturbed, and uncertain. He looked around to see if there was anyone else wishing to speak. Then from the back of the crowd Sujata, a woman in her thirties with a baby in her arms, stepped forward. She could hardly hold back her emotion. It took her a few moments to gather her composure. Everybody's eyes were upon her. Sujata wore a black sari indicating death and mourning. Her body was bereft of all ornaments. Her sad, almond-shaped eyes were filled with tears. Everyone knew who she was: a widow whose husband had been a poet, and whose magical songs had mesmerized the entire nation. But Angulimala brutally killed him, just in order to adorn his finger necklace.

The Law Officer stared at Angulimala full of hatred, thinking that the testimony of Sujata would be bound to bring a harsh sentence on the murderer. Surely the King would see that Sujata had been deprived of her beloved husband, the little baby had been made fatherless, and the nation had lost its treasured poet. This was the most heinous crime committed: this was a murder most despicable. There could be no pardon for such an evil deed.

Sujata's short silence seemed like an eternity. Then a soft voice was heard. She said, "I have been sitting here agonizing about my predicament. The loss of my husband has left me and my baby desolate. The scars of this crime will be with us until the end of our lives. My husband's spirit haunts me. I am unable to sleep, unable to eat, and it is so hard to live each day without him. But at the same time I am astonished to see such a turnaround in Angulimala; an avowed criminal is sitting among us with shaven head, transformed into a saint. It is difficult to come to terms with this situation. I have never encountered anything like this ever before."

Sujata stopped to breathe deeply. The Law Officer looked confused, wondering what was coming next. But the King looked relaxed, he wanted Sujata to say more and share her profound dilemma with the assembly.

"Your Majesty, on the one hand I wish to see Angulimala severely punished and made an example for others. On the other hand I think that Angulimala's death will not bring my husband back to life. I ask myself, what will be the benefit of one more death, and what will I and my child gain from it?"

Again Sujata paused. The audience was amazed to hear these words. The King waited in anticipation. The Law Officer looked away. These were not the words he wanted to hear from Sujata.

"Please continue," requested the King.

"Your Majesty, it may be true that Angulimala has genuinely changed, and I trust the sages when they say so. I see no sign of violence in his eyes. To ask for his death in this situation would be merely an act of revenge. I do not wish to be a part of it. I can imagine my husband saying that Angulimala's example gives hope to those who have committed crimes and who are either languishing in jail or who have been driven underground. Angulimala's example shows that no one is beyond redemption."

Sujata burst into a flood of tears. Nandini, sitting beside her, got up to console her.

Those who were unconvinced by the idealism of Mahavira and the Buddha warmed to the words of Sujata. If Sujata is prepared to forgive, they thought, then the rest of us must follow her. Sujata's sorrow, filled with longing and dignity, was spellbinding.

The Law Officer sensed that he was isolated. The King caught the mood of the gathering. He saw an openness and receptivity in the gathered crowd, and said:

"Gautama, the Buddha, and Mahavira, the Jina, are the most enlightened beings of our time, and we thank them both for extending our horizons. After due consideration and having heard all the arguments presented today, and particularly the sincere speech of Sujata, I avail myself of the Royal Prerogative and declare an amnesty for Angulimala. I pardon him. I am convinced that his renunciation of violence is genuine and his example will help others to renounce violence. What one person, the Buddha, has achieved, my entire army could not, so I offer my gratitude to the Buddha. Mahavira, your example of inclusion and integrity is also a great inspiration to us all. I also thank the learned sages and sadhus who have shown their generosity of spirit in being part of this occasion. Thank you all. Citizens of Savatthi, let us make this day a day of healing and reconciliation, a day of new beginnings and new hope. Last but not least, here is a bowl for donations to support and help those who have lost their loved ones. Please give generously. Thank you for coming."

The King himself made an offering of one thousand gold coins. Soon the pot was full.

Even though not everyone agreed with the King and his amnesty, they accepted it, and appreciated the wisdom and open-heartedness of the King.

After that remarkable assembly, Gautama the Buddha, together with Ahimsaka, began the great work of eradicating caste discrimination, especially the stigma of untouchability. They taught that all human beings, whatever their birth, have red blood and salty tears, and all of them have a desire to live and be happy; there is no ground for discrimination on the basis of birth. Many so-called low caste and untouchables took refuge in the Buddha and became monks; many others were given land and new sources of livelihood by the King. The Buddha and Ahimsaka inspired thousands upon thousands of people to seek inner peace and live in harmony with themselves and with all their fellow living beings, both humans and other than humans, by cultivating reverence, compassion, and loving-kindness.

CHAPTER SEVEN

From Death
to Life

One morning, Ahimsaka took up his begging bowl and set out for Savatthi. On the wayside near the Jeta Grove he saw a woman in labor lying down under a tree, panting and crying out. The young woman accompanying her was unable to do anything to help. Ahimsaka could not pass by, but not knowing what would be the duty of a monk in such a situation, he rushed to the Buddha for guidance.

"Blessed One, there is a woman in great pain, having difficulty in giving birth. What can I do?"

"Help her. Say to her, 'I have never harmed or killed anyone; by the merit and the power of my purity, I bless you. May you give birth with ease and peace.'"

The Buddha waited to hear Ahimsaka's reaction.

"Enlightened One, how can I honestly say that? You know I have taken so many lives and harmed so many people."

"I am pleased to see your mindfulness. You have passed the test. The merit of your truthfulness will certainly help the woman. Please say to her, 'Since I have taken refuge in Buddha I have renounced all violence—mental, verbal, and physical. If my nonviolence is genuine, then with my prayers and blessings may your birth be eased, and may you and your child be well.'"

Ahimsaka took leave of the Buddha and returned to the woman, who was still in great pain and crying out even louder. Ahimsaka was overcome with deep compassion and said, "Sister, since I have taken up the life of a wandering mendicant I have followed the way of the Buddha. If my commitment is genuine, if it is true, and if compassion has become part of my inner being, then may the power of my love help you to give birth with ease, and may you be free of pain and suffering."

Listening to the loving voice of Ahimsaka and feeling his radiant presence, the woman relaxed. Seeing that his soothing words were being effective, Ahimsaka continued, "Sister, the mother of my master, the Enlightened Buddha, was also traveling while pregnant and gave birth holding on to a tree."

The woman reached up and took hold of a low branch just above her.

"Sister, pain is part of life. By accepting it, its intensity is reduced. Do not resist it. Resistance to pain brings tension and anxiety, anxiety leads to fear. Fear of pain is worse than pain itself. This pain will pass. There is no need to fear, you are not alone, I am here. I offer you my life and my love for your well-being."

Ahimsaka's support helped to ease the woman's pain, and she gave birth safely to a beautiful baby. Ahimsaka, who as Angulimala had taken so many lives, now helped to bring new life into the world. Then and there Ahimsaka became enlightened. A terrorist became a buddha.

Ahimsaka gave up his midday meal. He stayed there until late in the afternoon. When the woman recovered from giving birth, she sat against the tree holding the baby in her arms.

"How good it is to see you and your baby doing well," said Ahimsaka. Then he reflected, and felt grateful that the Buddha had given him permission to witness the birth. He could have said, "Ahimsaka, mind your own business, go and bring food. Life is full of pain and suffering. Do not involve yourself in the affairs of the world." But he did not. The Enlightened One is truly compassionate.

The woman was pleased to see Ahimsaka still standing there, even though the hours were passing and the time for his midday meal had long gone. She said, "Monk, I am grateful to you for being with me, but aren't you supposed to keep aloof? Have I distracted you from your spiritual path?"

Ahimsaka was surprised at the woman's interrogation. Not long ago she had been crying out for help, but now she was able to raise religious questions. He answered, "No, it is not a distraction. I asked for guidance from the Buddha himself; he instructed me to use the merits of my spirituality to bless you. It is my calling to help all living beings gain deliverance from pain, whether physical or mental."

"But aren't you supposed to follow the path of nonattachment?" the woman wondered.

"Yes, we do. But it doesn't mean that we sit in meditation in the monastery all day, having no concern for the world. Nonattachment does not mean noncaring, inaction, or nonengagement. We cannot work toward the liberation of all living beings while remaining disengaged and aloof," answered Ahimsaka.

"But then how does it differ from attachment?"

"Attachment means clinging, being tied to a person or a place or an idea. Engagement is to realize that we are all related and connected, yet we are not bound to each other. There is no possessiveness in my heart; I am not 'I,' and nothing is 'mine.' Detached from desire and craving for personal gain and gratification, we monks act from compassion, not out of attachment," said Ahimsaka.

The woman was in no state to go deep into philosophical investigation. She stopped talking and rested. Ahimsaka did not wish to leave her alone.

"Are you feeling stronger?" asked Ahimsaka.

"Yes, I am," said the mother, while trying to breastfeed the newborn. "What a relief it is now that I feel no pain."

"I understand, sister, but only a living body can experience pain and only a living heart can experience sorrow. A dead body and a dead heart know nothing of pain and sorrow. The existence of pain is a fundamental truth of life. The art of living is in not magnifying or exaggerating sorrow; not allowing it to linger beyond its natural course. We need not hold on to it. When it is gone, it is gone. This is exactly the experience you have been through just now. The state of bliss is born from such equanimity. You have gone through such an experience."

As Ahimsaka was speaking, a carriage drew near him. It was Nandini on her way to visit the

Buddha. What synchronicity! She stopped the carriage when she saw Ahimsaka along the path—and she was happy to take the baby and the mother to their home.

AFTERWORD

❖ ◉ ❖

by Allan Hunt Badiner

Among all the experiences of the Buddha, perhaps his eye-to-eye encounter with an actual terrorist is the one most relevant and vital for those of us caught in the binds of the early twenty-first century. By telling the tale of the pitiless, blood-splattered Angulimala, Satish Kumar reminds us that when the Buddha deliberately and compassionately faced real fear, the fear in that real face evaporated. He has done a great service.

When the King learns in chapter two that the new monk whose teaching skills he finds so impressive is none other than the murderer his entire kingdom has been seeking to kill, he faints. Afterward, the King will realize, "What one person, the Buddha, has achieved, my entire army could not."

Soon a crowd went to the King and protested that Lady Nandini and the Buddha were harboring a terrorist. "Either they are with us or they are against us," cried the crowd. Luckily, the leadership in Savatthi thousands of years ago was wiser than that with which we find ourselves burdened today. The temptation to confuse evil and ignorance was ultimately resisted. Angulimala was himself the best example for his teachings—that people are best influenced by persuasion and, above all, example, as opposed to persecution.

By its end, this story of the transformation of Angulimala into Ahimsaka demonstrates that all human beings are connected by the profound desire to live and be cared for by others. It also reveals the counterintuitive, "against the grain" wisdom of the

Buddha, reminding us how Buddhist practice is a way to see that what we think is the "truth" is often the exact shadow opposite of what is really true.

Like Milarepa, who a millennium later transformed himself from a vengeful sorcerer into a saintly yogi, Angulimala morphed in one lifetime from a determined murderer into a devout protector of life, highlighting the basic Buddhist belief in impermanence and the endless possibilities of change. Ahimsaka became known as a conqueror of the "terrorist within," a tamer of the enemies inside oneself, and eventually a great *arahant,* or enlightened being.

Today, inspired by Angulimala, there are prison programs that teach meditation to inmates in Europe, Australia, and India. His transformation still inspires hope that even the terrorists of today—whether stateless murderers on the run or leaders of governments—can face the fear that lies within, and begin the healing of themselves and others.

Satish Kumar was born in India. He has studied Buddhism and was a Jain monk for nine years. He is the editor of *Resurgence* magazine and the director of programs at Schumacher College in England. He is the author of two other books, *No Destination: An Autobiography* and *You Are, Therefore I Am: A Declaration of Dependence*.

Thomas Moore, the author of the classic *New York Times* bestsellers *Care of the Soul* and *Soulmates*, lectures and writes about psychology, mythology, and the imagination. He lived as a monk in a Catholic religious order for twelve years and has degrees in theology, musicology, and philosophy.

Allan Hunt Badiner is a contributing editor at *Tricycle: The Buddhist Review* and an ecological activist. He is the coeditor of *Zig Zag Zen* and the editor of *Dharma Gaia, Mindfulness in the Marketplace* and other books.